To Paris Never Again

BOOKS BY AL PURDY

Poetry:

The Enchanted Echo (1944)
Pressed on Sand (1955)
Emu, Remember! (1956)
The Crafte So Long to Lerne (1959)
The Blur in Between: Poems 1960–61
    (1962)
Poems for All the Annettes (1962)
The Cariboo Horses (1965)
North of Summer: Poems from Baffin
    Island (1967)
Wild Grape Wine (1968)
Love in a Burning Building (1970)
The Quest for Ouzo (1971)
Hiroshima Poems (1972)
Selected Poems (1972)
On the Bearpaw Sea (1973)
Sex and Death (1973)
In Search of Owen Roblin (1974)
The Poems of Al Purdy: A New
    Canadian Library Selection (1976)
Sundance at Dusk (1976)
A Handful of Earth (1977)
At Marsport Drugstore (1977)
Moths in the Iron Curtain (1977)
No Second Spring (1977)
Being Alive: Poems 1958–78 (1978)
The Stone Bird (1981)
Birdwatching at the Equator: The
    Galapagos Islands (1982)
Bursting into Song: An Al Purdy
    Omnibus (1982)
Piling Blood (1984)
The Collected Poems of Al Purdy
    (1986)
The Woman on the Shore (1990)
Naked With Summer in Your Mouth
    (1994)
Rooms for Rent in the Outer Planets
    (1996)

Editor:

The New Romans: Candid Canadian
    Opinions of the US (1968)
Fifteen Winds: A Selection of Modern
    Canadian Poems (1969)
Milton Acorn, *I've Tasted My Blood:*
    Poems of 1956–1968 (1969)
Storm Warning: The New Canadian
    Poets (1971)
Storm Warning 2: The New Canadian
    Poets (1976)
Andrew Suknaski, *Wood Mountain*
    Poems (1976)

Other:

No Other Country (prose, 1977)
The Bukowski / Purdy Letters
    1964–1974: A Decade of Dialogue
    (with Charles Bukowski, 1983)
Morning and It's Summer: A Memoir
    (1983)
The George Woodcock / Al Purdy
    Letters (edited by George Galt,
    1987)
A Splinter in the Heart (novel, 1990)
Cougar Hunter (essay on Roderick
    Haig-Brown, 1993)
Margaret Laurence–Al Purdy: A
    Friendship in Letters (1993)
Reaching for the Beaufort Sea: An
    Autobiography (1993)
Starting from Ameliasburgh: The
    Collected Prose of Al Purdy (1995)

to Paris never again

NEW POEMS

AL PURDY

HARBOUR PUBLISHING

Harbour Publishing
P.O. Box 219
Madeira Park, BC V0N 2H0

Edited for the press by Sam Solecki.

Published with the assistance of the Canada Council and the Province of British Columbia through the British Columbia Arts Council.

Printed and bound in Canada.

Canadian Cataloguing in Publication Data

Purdy, Al, 1918–
    To Paris never again

    Poems.
    ISBN 1-55017-173-9

    I. Title.
PS8531.U8T6 1997   C811'.54   C97-910755-5
PR9199.3.P8T6 1997

THE CANADA COUNCIL | LE CONSEIL DES ARTS
FOR THE ARTS | DU CANADA
SINCE 1957 | DEPUIS 1957

For Eurithe

CONTENTS

LAMENT FOR BUKOWSKI

It isn't only the Great Bards
who "perne in a gyre"
believe in "the dark gods"
and court the Muse
wearing condoms:
it's also a guy
in his undershirt scoffing
a hot dog and 6-pack
in a crummy LA bedroom
betting a $350 horse
losing on a hundred dollar whore
and watching "the golden men
who push the buttons
of our burning universe"
and writing it all down

Well Buk
sometimes at least
you wrote like God with a toothache
cursing the whores cursing the horses
cursing the world
and blessing
something you rarely mentioned
hovering behind the scenes
there by indirection
your exact opposite:
Mozart dying alone in Vienna
quicklime over his body
snowflakes falling gently on Franklin's men
the frozen world so beautiful
there was nothing else in life
except what they dreamed was death
the King of the Jews on his cross
composing dirty limericks for Pop
—Bukowski in his coffin
dead as hell
but reaching hard for a last beer
and just about making it

To Paris Never Again

Looking for Sartre
and Simone de Beauvoir
at the Café Deux Maggots
looking for Voltaire
in bookstalls along the Seine
looking for Van Gogh
to say I loved him
finding only fleas
racing round my midsection
stomach upset from the water
turning over and over
every half hour
drinking only wine

Rounding a corner suddenly
to confront Audrey Hepburn
(which is nice confronting)
and her new husband Mel Ferrer
I had read in English papers
they were on their honeymoon
and had a kind of glow
that marks some newlyweds
it was like finding a story
on the Paris sidewalk

At the Louvre
moving from painting to painting
I began to lose the sense of reality
from these larger-than-life
people and places
expecting to see Pierre Bonnard
sneaking in to retouch his paintings
when the guard wasn't looking
and me acting suspiciously

Before you speak to someone
they look at you knowingly
betrayed without a word
into being a foreigner

and thought American
—at least half of Paris
sitting somewhere
in front of street cafes
old men playing chess
other old men
searching for cigarette butts
old men wise as encyclopedias
old women who once knew Casanova

I want so much to be in love here
but no one to be in love with
and finding an emotion
shimmering like a pearl
lost near the Arc de Triomphe
by a despairing lover
it's copyright and belongs
to someone else
I left it there
in the gutter shimmering

A room near the Metro
with the noise of trains
a vibration in your bones
of such an intensity
it sucks you out of bed
dreaming of Marie Antoinette
and Eleanor of Aquitaine
in a castle the size of Alberta
joining the other scared passengers
clutching their transfers
and wake up sleepwalking

Before leaving Canada
I'd stayed with Irving Layton
a man so positive of himself
he'd exposed all my negatives
and in this most glamorous city
in the world I wandered
around not knowing who I was
tramping the Rue Pigalle

and Montmartre
at the Tuilleries and Odeon
making notes for poems
pretending to be a writer
then returning to London
back to Canada
—and after a long time
finally beginning to understand
the man in my head was me

TRAVEL ARTICLE

We get most of the details
about those stone-age people
in the Orkney Islands
five thousand years ago:

"one skull has teeth blunted
from long-term chewing
of grain to make home brew
or perhaps leather to soften it"

"the most common life span
between 15 and 30 years"

"an indent across the top
of a young woman's skull
caused by the leather strap
of a basket she used to carry
slung from her head"

I wonder about that young woman
what her life was like
—the basket she had to lug around
like an old-man-of-the-sea
riding her shoulders & becoming
part of her everyday identity
and think of the breathless sounds
she made in her lover's arms
the sounds we all make *in extremis*
and did her back ache sometimes
from doing so much kitchen work
and work men think beneath them
did she look for meaning in her life
and perhaps the end was a relief
not the beginning of nothing
—but could it be possible
she found something so beautiful
she was able to take a holiday
from knowing she had to die
nearly five thousand years ago

somewhere close to happiness
a holiday in the secret place
she had discovered inside herself?

AFTER THE WAR

Late in the Bronze Age:
guardsmen lounging at the Lion Gate
discussing Helen's sexual preferences
what happened to Priam's family
laughing about the Wooden Horse
scratching their fleas
—in his marble bath
Agamemnon King of Mycenae
washing off the dust of travel
on his return from Troy
and mulling over his confrontation
in the Troad with mankiller Achilles
an argument over some slave girls
and gazing into those uncanny eyes
his own fear and the difficulty
of continuing to stand there
pretending to be King Agamemnon
the idea of himself wavering
—then noticed an odd reflection
in the water—it seemed like
a sunbeam dancing on the water
then became a flashing sword
hovering at his shoulder
his wife and her lover
—then one long moment passed
a moment filled with centuries
while the Furies buzzed
about the bloody bathwater
like fruit flies

A JOB IN WINNIPEG

That summer we hated each other
the gender wars ablaze
brief gunfire then silence
she left me to stay with friends her face
twitching fiercely

—summer's end
maple sumac poplar yellow and red
sunrise and sunset leaped at the sky
joined at the navel like a huge
McDonald's hamburgers logo
above the house we built together
I moped from room to room and mourned
the broken marriage and my own mistakes
all things seemed to say goodbye
and I enjoyed my own mournfulness
—outside
muskrats pushed the lake ahead of them
with their noses like marathon swimmers
black squirrels were permanent voyeurs
at screens and windows until
I began to feel like a black squirrel a little
and a naked woman smiled at me her body
covered with red sores like blossoms
I kept dreaming about her
in the cedar-scented night
            in pine-smelling evenings
she prowled through my veins
            like a diseased goddess
and I
Homo Erectus in the woodshed

—afternoons
I wandered Norris Whitney's woods
thumbing my nose at him
and the shotgun he had for trespassers
trying not to enjoy the autumn colours
for that would mean my marriage wasn't serious
but it was by God it was

16

and I am completely bewildered by myself
by my own ruses to avoid pain
and the syllogism I'd figured out
about life had only two parts
and "therefore"
went wandering alone in the desert
trying to complete a *ménage à trois*

—the great pike have sunk into deep water
rabbits search for underground apartments
butterflies decamped for Mexico
birds likewise
and the son of man hath nowhere
       to lay his head
except Winnipeg where there's a job waiting
and if I set my mind to it
I can do without Winnipeg
—I think there must be a spell laid on me
by some god or other
and I've got to stop this facetious voice
hysteric metrics
that I hear going on and on
destroying everything that's important
genuine feeling and emotions
I'm hurt and laughing about it
which is silly
for I know the pain is real
which might mean that I am not real
at which the trees and moon and sky
waver and fade waver and fade
and maybe Winnipeg wavers too
right before my eyes and I pass my hand
completely through
what I thought was a tree
and swear it's a tree
but I'm standing on the planet
which is myself
seeing only my shadow self
dancing on a cave wall
in a kind of semaphore
visible to no one

TRAVEL NOTES: CROSSING THE PRAIRIES

—9/10ths of the landscape is sky
more sunlit heaven than earth
except for the engine's profane roar
and I have the illusion
there's nothing at all under the car
no rich soil capable of producing
40 bushels to the acre instantly
just wheels spinning and spinning
in empty air
sky a colossal white glare
nearly a vacuum
except for the shrivelled brown bug
that's us
scrambling to escape the light

—no renaissance cathedral no hammering
crescendo of 647 airliners
heralding the Second Coming
could dominate this landscape
only a mad imaginary god
shrieks and shrieks in human ears
Saskatchewan

I was unable to join them
in that unknown country
where people were made of glass
and you saw their hearts beating
in the mirror of memory
and I have invented
imaginary souls for them
that kept on living when they died
and think their thoughts for them

There was Enid
once when I asked for ketchup
to use on a delicate recipe of hers
she was so angry with me
I was delighted and loved her for it
—she told me a story about an Irish tinker
and another about an aristocrat in Ireland
who lost a wager over a thoroughbred horse
and rather than relinquish the beautiful animal
he killed it
a different kind of creature
it couldn't realize what being owned meant
—and Enid wept a moment
        in the hot afternoon
        of southern Florida
four thousand miles from Ireland
And Tom
years ago when he was especially boring
and I was taking pride in my bad manners
I told him so and he said
"I hope that won't make any difference
to our friendship"
which till then I hadn't known existed
but after that it did
—one of those people partly invisible
and after you understand
about the missing parts of them
you begin to see the others
where they hadn't been noticed before

And Hilda
a warmth about her
and yet so contained in herself
you could know only about sixty percent
she consented that you know
—on a holiday back in Germany
at her relatives' party
she showed up in a clown suit
red nose white cheeks blue chin
a stranger to all her relations
they wondered where she came from
and didn't know the clown
and Bill
who left a note for me in a book that said
I'll wait for you in the west
Till your sun comes down for its setting
And the world has become darker now
And Milton
who was not content in life
in earth he has forgotten
the earth
and that being there might be happiness
if he had known what it was
—then please tell me someone
"What is happiness
that is gone before you remember?"

all these and more

—go where the wandering waters go
all the way home

Muss i Denn

Six of us at the dinner table
in sociable converse
and German baritone
Erich Kunz
belting out a drinking song
on the record player
when my friend David
himself a strong baritone
starts to accompany Kunz
but translating the German words
to English as he goes along
and they sing a duet
in two languages
                    the machine
with a man inside and the man
who is not a machine
and the table talk
stops

—a full six seconds removed
from the texture of time
not recorded by clocks
the world rotating without us
who are under a spell
with little manikins dancing
inside our bodies
with small conductors
waving passionate batons
and a few helpers
we keep inside our heads
for household duties
to lay out our thoughts
for us and remind us
of things have stopped
reminding us of things

—during that lost time
old kingdoms have gone to ruin
fragments of silence

trapped in crumbling walls
and time enough for the wind
to pause and whisper
a secret to the river
something about
a water nymph
who was once human
and time enough
for every secret
to be forgotten

BRUEGEL'S *ICARUS*

—a ten-year-old boy
escapee from the island of Crete
with a child's delight in having wings
exploring the endless blue sky
argonaut of Cirrus and Cumulus
brave as Jason and Theseus
in a discovery of eagles
flying over Samos Delos and Paros
over drowned valleys of rivers
and seas like upside-down skies
then bewildered by the sun
navigation all screwed-up
heading west by mistake
and down in the sea
off Bruegel's Flanders
"a boy falling out of the sky"
in Auden's poem drowning far
from home: in the painting
the ploughman with eyes only
for keeping a straight furrow
and the "expensive delicate ship" with
perishable cargo too busy to launch
a lifeboat goes about its business
making more profits for investors
—and Daedalus the boy's father
giving up the search as hopeless
turns east for Sicily

—off to one side of the painting
a dead body in nearby woods
which everyone managed to ignore
and one wonders why since dead bodies
left in woodlots are generally those
of murdered men or raped women
and cops very scarce

(—a school text footnote
supplies this dead body info
some black squiggles on paper

repeated in other books
a print run of ten thousand say
and I therefore deceive myself
into thinking I've made a discovery
not mentioned by Auden
the result of this self deception being
like a flower in my mind
the footnote blossoms)

—questions:
did someone in authority say
"Round up the usual suspects"?
and where did the victim come from
and who knocked him off
and where did the killer get to
and were the equivalents of Sam Spade
and Philip Marlowe in charge of the case?
—one can't help feeling
Bruegel had someone special in mind
for victim in that painting
and the body wasn't just his invention
a man who didn't show up
for breakfast and lunch next day
one of those "Hunters in the Snow"
trudging wearily homeward
gun slung across his shoulders
or a cook in his "Peasant Wedding"
mixing up a nice batch of poison
—or has the murderer escaped
sneaking off with bloody fingers
just beyond the painting's edge
entering a different reality
his genetic inheritors
named Bernardo and Clifford Olson
or maybe an unknown someone
sitting next to you on Air Canada
(more than one myth operating here)
walking behind you late at night
the sound of his steps echoing
pursuer and pursued
and which are you?

—but another image
persists in my mind:
just before drowning
a scared little boy
a long way from home
crying for his mother

ODE TO A DEAD BURRO

What is it that shakes one
from the "even tenor of our ways"
that brings home mortality
and says even the small is valuable
a grassblade may touch a grassblade
one trivial thing connects with another
and a glance has special poignancy?

One night in a farmer's cornfield
in Mexico a volcano was born
with a little red devil sitting
on top yelling "God is dead"
to everyone listening
—this was in 1943 at Paricutin
when lava drowned one village
then another
and surrounded a church
but perhaps with God's help
the church survived
while 4000 people fled in terror
and fire screamed at the world

In 1979 we visited the volcano
1700 feet high and now dormant
—the soil black for miles around
but people had returned long ago
having lost their fear of the dead thing
—our party rented burros for the women
and one of the animals was lame
I remembered that much later
when my own feet gave me trouble

thinking about the lame burro
of little use to its owner
for much longer in 1979
and would die soon anyway
this memory returning from the silence
surrounding all of us
how precarious our lives are

(trivia connects with trivia)
the desolation in our hearts
the blade of grass soon withered
—and for our own loves
now and in future
for the dust columns of refugees
and the already dead
lying alone in the rain
the world's grief and our own
become too large to handle—:
in lieu of that overwhelming sorrow
that we must feel to be human
(if we are human)
spend a small amount of sadness
on a dead burro in Mexico
if you find that possible

—climbing a mountain road
in low gear
the transport in front stopped
suddenly so we did too
glimpsing a stake truck
rounding a curve ahead
and racing downhill toward us
its brakes failed
—and I had the illusion
that all movement ended
that speeding truck
and ourselves were both
double-parked on the road
right beside each other
and I saw their faces
trapped inside the cab
like in a funeral parlour
with us just across the street
in *our* parlour window
before dying
and their distorted faces
stared at me:
a boy with stiff pale face
like a turn-of-the-century photo
his mouth wide open
a man with white bald head
the sun hadn't touched
brown underneath where it had
he was sneering at the windshield
or seeming to
as if he found the world
all around us hateful
and a woman with eyes closed
soundlessly praying
in a kind of trance
—my brain empty of feeling
except stunned helplessness
for they were strangers to me
and how does one love a stranger

except he become a friend?
—anyway
the truck went crashing
far down the mountainside
disintegrating as it went
the transport in front stayed put
but knowing the habits of Mexican police
with witnesses to an accident
I drove around it
silently up the mountain
My silence a bit self-protective
thinking about that little
rat-like mammal who was
successor to the dinosaurs
that eventually became us
at least I would have been
thinking that if I'd thought of it
but I wasn't

THE GODS OF NIMRUD DAG

On my workroom wall: a large colour photograph
from an English Sunday paper: stone heads of gods
on top of a Turkish mountain called Nimrud Dag.
It gives me a weird feeling to glance at it,
and find blank stone eyes staring back at me.
These heads have a majesty that surpasses their
non-existence in any other form than sculpture.
One of them, ten feet tall and facing the camera,
has an expression that might be indifference;
or it might be an emotion entirely unknown
to humans. You look and begin to understand
now the way the old ones felt then,
when a graven image belched fire,
and a spirit presence touched your face.
These were the gods of our fathers:
they are not to be dismissed from our own lives,
even if we worship no longer at their shrines
—an unused part of the brain knows them,
when the priests' chanting dies
and the moon silent on the silent mountain.

MARIUS BARBEAU: 1883–1969

In 1968
a little old man dancing
at home near downtown Ottawa
demonstrating western Indian dances
out of courtesy to a visitor—:

wearing a feathered headdress
and beaded buckskin jacket
ducking his head and beating a drum
chanting *HI-yah HI-yah HI-yah*
the sound part animal part human
circling the dark dinner table
and old-fashioned sideboard
his feet tremulous
age too much for him
—then something happened
something invisible to me
and he seemed to gather strength
perhaps remembering Rocher de Boule
the mountain at the end of the sky
his body weaving among shadow totems
of Kitwanga and Kitwankool
gathering to himself and of himself
Tsimsyan and Gitksan people
villages of the mountains
and rivers of the valleys
Skeena and Nass flowing swiftly
past legs of the dining room table
—his face a tranced dream face
having forgotten his visitor
chanting and beating the drum,
he danced himself into silence

Remembering that time
I was slightly embarrassed for him
now I'm embarrassed that I was embarrassed
and faintly in my own lifetime
have glimpsed the shining mountains

see myself staggering through deep snow
lugging blocks of wood yesterday
an old man
almost falling from bodily weakness
—look down on myself from above
then front and both sides
white hair—wrinkled face and hands
it's really not very surprising
that love spoken by my voice
should be when I am listening
ridiculous
yet there it is
a foolish old man with brain on fire
stumbling through the snow

—the loss of love
that comes to mean more
than the love itself
and how explain that?
—a still pool in the forest
that has ceased to reflect anything
except the past
—remains a sort of half-love
that is akin to kindness
and I am angry remembering
remembering the song of flesh
to flesh and bone to bone
the loss is better

MACHU PICCHU
—in the Peruvian Andes

Like being surrounded
by menacing picture postcards
standing on end
an overwhelmingness of stone
a thunder in the vision
—ghosts of Incas so absent here
and I so aware of them
their absence a negative-plus
—and next morning the neighbouring
mountain Birney once climbed
completely mist-obscured
and perhaps he is still climbing
from his Toronto hospital room
and if I yell "Hi Earle"
I'll hear his Andean bellow
"Come on up Al"
—only one thing to do
in a place like thunder and lightning
stand and rejoice
that you're alive in the mountains
for as long as may be
and to have all these things
fizz in your head like cheap booze
is using up all your quota
of inexhaustible delight
—that life should bring such gifts
and wrap them in clouds and stars

THE EYES OF MILDRED TREGILLUS

—at the end of the research
for my BC ghost towns article
I had to see this elderly lady
at the Quesnel extended care facility
—the place made me a bit nervous
like I was treading on teacups
or tromping on lace doilies
and said to the nurse "Oh don't
wake her up—I'll come back later"
and the nurse said just like a nurse
"She'll want to see her visitor
—they just *live* for visitors"
so I feel better like a kinda
private benefactor or something
—name of Tregillus
eyes alert and intelligent
but scarcely older than me
(I wondered how she'd feel
about changing places)
dark hair on the white pillow
and awake as stars are awake
late in the night sky
and I said something about
her father and brother being miners
and how talking about their lives
would help me write my own piece
she looked me over quietly
and said "There are no stories"

I was seen through
and through like a clear window
straight into my mind
like starlight in the mind
Tregillus looked and judged
all my adult disguises useless
grey hair and years stripped off
birth-naked
and I am seized with embarrassment
for being an insensitive lout

my self-love vanished
and all this came upon me in silence
then like an enormous clock striking
deep in eternity
—I scurry out of there
(avoiding Tregillus' eyes)
to be alone with myself
to somehow rebuild what I am
and it is growing late

UNTITLED

I am waiting for time to come
holding the many days' sameness inside me
fold on fold of invisible stuff
that you can't see and yet piles up
secretly in the mind like nothing at all
an unseen dust
—then I ask myself what I'm talking about
and can't answer that either:
a quantity of something I can't describe
or measure or prove or disprove

—but there is something
that keeps me from madness:
for the astronomers have told us
about an unexplained "wobble"
an eccentricity of movement
in the orbits of certain stars
which predicates the existence
of an invisible something
some kind of spatial presence
which can be measured and calibrated
and they attempt to describe it

—this stuttering little story of mine
has nothing to do with science
except make an inadequate parallel:
my own blood leaps sometimes
in its arterial voyaging
its circular journey to nowhere
when the spirit seen by no human
makes its presence known
and I can't describe its "wobble"
other than to say there is a loveliness
my heart knows

THE CLEVER DEVICE

Time that is
weightless & colourless & invisible
and measurable
by little tick-tock noises
of the heart sinking into
eternity for the last time

Time that is measurable
by a handful of sand
passing through a narrow place
in the hourglass skeleton
—an idiot face
peering from the basement
windows of your soul

Time is a thing you invented
for a point of reference
for yourself
—after three score years
and ten of your clever device
you point to yourself
in the mirror
and say POUF
you no longer exist
and laugh
or not be able to laugh

MINOR INCIDENT IN ASIA MINOR

It's a worrisome matter
every day in my workshop
I think about it
during the back and forth
motion of the handsaw
crosscutting timber
the grating sound
making my ears ache
—in silence at the tavern
everyone talking at once
until I enter the place
I glance at them
they turn away from me
and whisper to each other
my anger bubbling
—stopping work this morning
in a rare calm moment
to contemplate the shrinkage
in width of a green board
and the puzzle of relative
non-shrinkage in its length
invisibly in the night
the thing happens
which every carpenter
who ever lived
must be aware of
—then throw down my hammer
wander onto the barren plain
of Esdraelon at noonday
for a breath of air
a bird calling somewhere

Then the voices return
in tavern and street
the voices like raindrops
like poisoned rain
I hear them continually
around the corner
somebody talking

just beyond hearing
somebody saying things
I don't want to know
and cannot escape:
my young wife a virgin
but pregnant yes pregnant
a word that offends me
but I cannot escape it
and supernaturally pregnant
by some other "person"
and not by her husband?
—by a god then
by a goddamned god

The wine-bibbers watch me
for a sign that I know
what they think they know
that she is no longer a virgin
I watch her belly day by day
for some hint or clue
eager yet apprehensive
of what she may bring forth
Yesterday one of the village
ne'er-do-wells taunted me
about the rumours
stood in my face and said
Cucklold Cuckold
and a great rage came over me
I leaped for him
left him on his back pleading
he didn't mean anything
then went home and drank wine

I cannot ask her for the truth
maybe she does not know the truth
a young girl still and innocent
even when she is not innocent
and what does that mean?
—that she dreams reality
and cannot tell the difference
I have taken a fresh pine board

and laid it gently on her lap
and I say to her:

"The width of this board will shrink
and change but its length
is as it is and will remain
—so tell me then
is a god responsible for
the board's shrinkage the same
by whom it is said you are pregnant?
Or is that some other god?
And I who am your husband
the drunks mock me and call me
cuckold when I pass on the street
and will you leave me to go
with this god who has no name but god?
Who am I then in truth
that you should forsake me
for a god you have never seen
who comes to you only in darkness
and leaves at the first light
of whom you say 'I am chosen'?
Who am I then in the darkness
no man can escape
who am I when daylight comes?"

CASE HISTORY

—"the bad times"
after our A-frame house
was half-built in the 1950s:
I found odd jobs
collecting scrap iron
picking tomatoes
selling apples door to door
anything to make a buck
then we ran out of money
and things got desperate
for our small family of three
even food was a problem
at least a couple of times
we cooked road-killed rabbits
there were fish in the lake
neighbours gave us vegetables
and pitied my wife:
—then I discovered the garbage dump
near Mountainview RCAF base
it was Aladdin's open air cafe
and not much stink
with air force food rations
in little aluminum foil envelopes
powdered eggs milk coffee
dehydrated potatoes dried fruit
a treasure trove of calories
and a matter of some rejoicing
in our crippled financial condition
—during all this scavenging
the family unit of three
was a model of togetherness
careful not to show themselves
above the brow of the hill
in case of military cops
—and besides the bounteous food
boxes of various sizes
made of quarter-inch plywood
and gallon cans of paint
in black and red colours

some nearly half full
whereat we rejoiced greatly
and sang hosanna
on Mountainview garbage dump

—for the next few weeks
we feasted on the stuff
and it was of high quality
nothing but the best
for our boys in blue
(I'd been one of them myself
during the recent war)
and I worked on that plywood
fitted it to the living room floor
painted it artistically
like a huge checkerboard
in colours of black and red
—much later
when a high school gymnasium
was demolished in nearby Belleville
I bought the hardwood flooring cheaply
to cover my elegant checkerboard
and with literary confidence
I didn't really feel
stashed the worksheets of a poem
inside the house overhang
along with a note
directing future discoverers
to take the sheets to the English Dept.
of any Canadian university
and receive as reward
for this unknown masterpiece
one small case of beer
or more likely
an embarrassing question
"Purdy—who he?"

—during those house-building days
and for some time after
a strong feeling
of having touched existence itself

yet being myself no more
than a cloud shadow on earth
awake in the night
for a few moments
then falling asleep again
without remembering
—in winter going outside
completely naked
to meet myself in the night
with lake ice splitting
from shore to shore
a noise like forty dead men
all awakening at once
and shouting me dumb
northern lights
whispering down the sky
including me
in their silver rivers
cold so cold
water boils in my veins
and somewhere in the cedars
a bird is singing

—I say to myself
in wondering tones
is any of this exaggeration?
hoking it up a little?
—how else explain yourself to yourself
and do everything all over again
the way it was then
the way it was then

HER ILLNESS

Since Eurithe became ill
(more like damn sick)
she's growing more and more distant
from me at first it was
only in the next town
where somebody phoned to check
if I knew anyone with an odd name
when I arrived to pick her up
she was gone again this time
reported in Sutton Hoo
site of a Viking ship-burial
gazing contemplatively
at the excavation
getting farther away
in the festering heat of Africa
where Kurtz had been sighted
during the full moon
then it was made known to me
in a dream that she had arrived
on the ghostly companion of Sirius
and might have gone undetected
for centuries and I was alarmed
on accounta air is a bit thin there
then a faint wailing cry
like a bereavement of witches
(but she is notably undemonstrative)
coming from Betelgeuse
in the constellation Orion
and she is frightened
for bedbugs and dung-beetles there
engage in endless warfare

—this is what illness does
and I think from her expression
that she will never return to me

134 FRONT ST., TRENTON, ONT.

Entering my mother's house
six years after her death
when the will is finally probated—

The family portraits stare
all haunted by each other's likenesses
the parlour become a museum
and serious
for being dead is a serious matter
faces frozen for the camera
expressions fixed and unforgiving
as if they agreed with the trust company
that prevented settlement of the will
—under their eyes
I shrivel to a small boy again
awaiting my long-delayed punishment
it takes sunshine for my spirits to recover

Outside
the old red barn
in the backyard is gone
—when I was 12 or 13
I built a sailboat in that barn
it had a monster wooden keel
that I secured with steel shelf brackets
it wouldn't tack into the wind
and turned over near the town bridge
I had to be towed back to Bronson's dock
with people watching from the bridge
—that red barn
somebody on the town council
must have decided the world
was just as well off without a red barn
—there were ring bolts on the wall
from the time when horses lived there
a few wisps of ancient hay
stuck between boards
and strands of coarse hair

remaining when some impatient animal
switched its tail in small unhappiness

The maple tree in front is gone too
and once I thought that tree
was as old as the world
and came to believe
there was another country
hidden among its high branches
and I called from my bedroom window
to another kid in that green sky
and he became my friend
—my mother thought I was talking in my sleep
when she came into the bedroom
I snored a little

Upstairs
opening an old chest full of wool blankets
a cloud of moths explodes at me
like biblical locusts
thanking me for self-determination
and looking for something else to eat
—they would have dismayed my mother
so would the missing red barn
and vanished maple tree
standing bewildered in the doorway
"Everything looks so different" she would say
"Don't things look different to you dear?"
Yes they do
but I can't tell her the reason

My Grandfather

—a hundred years before
the flood before
Gilgamesh & Enkidu before
Gondwanaland & Laurasia before
God came out of the egg
and huffed and puffed and blew
Abraham out of Ur of the Chaldees
right about then my grandfather came by
and sniffed and said *Huh*
this place ain't nothin much
and love was born about then
on accounta things were so awful
what could you do
but fall in love with our only world

... yeast in the mud-pie
or was it a lightning
and ammonia cocktail
with maybe a soupçon
of spectral sunshine
to trigger chemicals
into one-celled creatures
tyrannosaurus monsters
and shrew-like mammals
then *Homo Erectus*
Leapfrogging continents
Africa to Asia
Asia to Europe
the wandering primate
early man
searching the hemispheres
to find a woman
deep as a well
then a long pause
of millions of lifetimes
between the rivers
Tigris and Euphrates
to create cuneiform
writing and mud houses
then the Ubaid period
(pale green pottery
with black designs)
Uruk and onward
the Sumer king-list
Gilgamesh et cetera
part man and part god
and things got interesting
with heroes and suchlike
philosophic questions
that remain unanswered
long after humans
inventing laughter
inventing God

invented themselves
and looked into a mirror ...

... a knowledge strikes home sometimes
full realization of the invisibly obvious:
we're all related to those people
potters and priests and farmers
scribes and armorers
        craftsmen and kings
all of us every one
and in rare moments of meditation
when I am naked to myself
it has seemed to me
that I have entered their craniums
my oneness become twoness and threeness
joining those long ago people
lodged in their multiple brains
immured there
unable to speak words
only see and listen
and sometimes understand
hidden in their brains' pulsing chambers
witness
in uncanny rose-coloured light
to the slow-evolving machinery
of human existence
moving from dim room to dim room
in whispering stillness
my own blood leaping
in the weirs and valves of their bodies
in the falls and rapids of their blood streams
              and theirs in mine
early in the human adventure
proceeding in zigzag disorderly fashion
from the impossible to the inevitable
from the Lascaux masters to Rilke
      then quite suddenly
      over the long millennia
quite suddenly
I become

... an apprentice in Kiangsi province
lying down to sleep in kiln dust
with a few snowflakes falling
thinking
    not of Chang Ch'ien sailing
    a log down the Milky Way
    or himself plunging into the fire
    to make a red bowl for
    some emperor
being only an apprentice
homesick for the wet green
of Kiangsi province
lying down to sleep in the hot dust ...

THE NAMES THE NAMES

I'm scared "they flee from me
that sometime did me seeke"
—George Margaret Milt John
Gus Tom—and suddenly
old age grabs cruel tight
I have to look em up in letters
to remember their names
then forget all over again
I think of the old farmer
who fondled his land
who loved what he thought it was
then both thought and reality
were taken from him
as my names are gone
I pursue them into darkness
follow the remembered faces
I've conjured in my head
by an act of will
they have no names attached
but light up when they see me
they smile with recognition
and depend on me for something
for something vital to all of us
our faces our faces but names
the names of my life are gone
and what am I but what I remember?
Well I remember Van Gogh's painting
the one with bursting stars
and whirling constellations at night
and a little provincial restaurant
at night in Van Gogh's head
the artist's head full of them
crowded with bursting stars
and think of my own lost skull
hairless skinless and yellowish
tucked away in some deserted
lonely unnoticed place
but full of Van Gogh's bursting lights
shining inside the empty abandoned thing

and full of those names the lost ones
the lost names returned at last to me

and the worms rejoice

SURGERY

It's a minor op
but facing the knife
under general anaesthetic
I will be again
as close to death
as I have been since the beginning
since before I was
feeling curious and apprehensive
venturing into barrier darkness
long enough to say Hello
to old friends
Earle Birney George Woodcock
and Milton Acorn
but that's not likely
I won't be far enough away
from the dark boundaries
a place of childhood monsters
from which one of my own kind
will rescue me
in all likelihood
drag me back
from there to here
in which case
I might have more to say
later on in another poem

ALDEN NOWLAN
MILTON ACORN
& PURDY

They hadn't seen each other
for a couple of years
when I shepherded them to a table
in the Blue Mountain restaurant
and ordered some beer
—three poets
all very different
Acorn and Nowlan talking away
about metrics in Periclean Athens
or something like that
but I couldn't understand a single word
not one
of what they were saying to each other
but think I know now
it was just that
they liked each other
this was their way of showing it
and this delighted me
I listened hard
Nowlan had had a throat operation
for cancer a few months ago
and kept going
        rubble rouble rabble
Acorn sounded like an about-to-be
extinct mastodon
he kept going
        gabble babble gargle
which seemed to be
a kind of bastard iambics
part of some completely unknown verse form
tho I couldn't be sure
and I started laughing
turning away so they wouldn't notice
when I switched my chair around
again they were both gone
I was sitting alone at the table
nursing a beer

but when I went to drink it
the bottle was empty
and the place getting dark
I sat there for quite a long time
thinking about the three of us
and slowly beginning to realize
that at least two of us
were dead

HELICOPTER

Straight up
just hovering
then bounce
then dance
against air
glide swoop dive
thru valleys
eroded mountains
unbarred for us
and machine is magic
machine is machine
machine is bird
eagle hawk falcon
anything but dove
follow the Peace
Halfway and Moberly
Rivers and out
of bare-boned aspens
trot white-assed elk
gallops a moose
charging air
Cameron River
Charley Creek
Hudson Hope
Dawson Creek
Kiskatinaw River
all of them
down toboggan slides
of rubbery air
over ski-jumps
of solid nothing
and below us
grey land ruin
broken dentures
of ancient forests
petroleum lakes
miles underneath
earth's navel stone
packed with centuries

millenniums eras
of bodies and bones
garbage of earth
five billion years
mammal mother
mammal father
reptile forefathers
press your face on it
your face in the earth
the place you came from
and eat your ancestors
spirit country
magic earth
east Atlantic
west Pacific
joined at the navel
by this strange country
and like a lead feather
we land in high wind
of our own making
avian creatures
avian humans
home

FORT ST. JOHN

ON THE BEACH
   —for Pat Lane

On the beach at Galilee
mending nets with Cousin Nathan
when this young fellow comes by
trailed by a bunch of other guys
"Nathan" I say "what you done
that they sent the cops for you?"
And the young fellow says to us
"Follow me follow me
and I will make you fishers of men—"
Now I've seen guys like this before
quite a few times before
and they was generally on the make
"Well what about it?" he says
"What about what?" I answer back
and it's a stalemate
"Are you coming with me?"
"Nope"
"What do you mean 'Nope'?"
"Whaddaya think I mean?"

That was a few months back
and the news just come from Jerusalem
how the Romans killed him
me wondering now why I said no
but the man is very dead
which is a very good reason
Other reasons as well:
he was a criminal of some kind
a thief of souls they say
and I would have lost myself
or some part of myself
it would have been taken from me

On the great lake of Galilee
at night I have studied the water
and stars that were the likeness of stars
shining on the water's surface
and thinking—am I a man

that I follow another man
as a sheep might follow
—a man in another man's likeness?
The rumour is he was more than a man
but many have that pretense
as if being what you are
is never enough

Well he is gone
and the sun still shines
by day on Galilee
at night the stars look down
and stars in the likeness of stars
shine on the water
I wish him well this man
who died
this man in the likeness of a god

HOUSE PARTY—1000 BC
    —*after Rilke*

A god standing in the doorway
and looking like everyone else
another late arrival at the party
until he speaks to King Admetus:
"You must die within the hour"
—no question of belief
or disbelief from anyone
the god could not be doubted

It was like Icarus falling
from the sky
when his wax wings melted
screaming all the way down
Admetus falling from his couch
screaming on the floor

"Unless" the god said looking
at the writhing body with distaste
"unless someone willingly dies
in your place—"
"willingly?" "instead of me?"
My friend Creon? Parents?
Wife? Alcestis?
Alcestis

The king's features collapsed
inward on themselves
like bubbles in hot soup
nose mouth eyes ears moved
from their places in his face
rearranging themselves
and twitching horribly
twitching
he became completely
a stranger to himself
and completely mad

The woman—really only a girl
her face becomes a screen
with pictures for thoughts
in which another self lived
a life within her life
so that all the house guests
she looked upon were dead long ago
and her thoughts were a grief for them
then changed from grief to sadness
the sadness of remembering
what her friends were like
and what her husband was like
when you can't feel any longer
and love for her husband was the ache
of not feeling love any longer
the ache of knowing what love had once been
knowing now only the imitation feeling
occupying the same place
remembering what it felt like
from the imitation inside herself
but not remembering very well
And now to die?
But the child?
What child?
—the child who does not yet exist
with doorways opening and closing somewhere
arrivals and departures
memento of herself in another body
the residue of a self gone elsewhere

All this time the god
has lingered in the doorway
his face changing and changing
—the parents bewildered
clinging to each other
in the way of old people
"What's going on here?"
affixed to their faces
Creon in deathly fear and hiding
behind a candelabra's silver flowers

Alcestis moves toward the god
who has joined the other guests
but they keep some distance away
and now remember his name
the messenger of the gods
Alcestis stops in puzzlement
something important was happening
and just one moment ago
she can't remember what it was
—the child—ah yes—the child
who cannot yet exist
but cries within her body to exist
Glancing back at her husband
and then at the god's changing face
which calls her to him
—so beautiful a face it is
that speaks of generations
in the far future
but nothing earthly added to itself
nothing earthly
so beautiful she thinks it is
and after that
the shining

Admetus watches them
the god and his wife who was
they are vanishing in light
rushing away from his guests
and from his own life
seeing them fade and give birth to light
and it is suddenly yesterday
then tomorrow
and none of these things happened
between yesterday and tomorrow
and now it is much too late
for anything but weeping
and he weeps
Admetus weeps

IN TURKEY

Crossing on the ferry from Rhodes
arriving bewildered without Turkish money
I brandish travellers cheques to a cop
in dumb show hoping he'll translate this
to money money money
he grins and points and we grin back
and catch a minibus north
with several other passengers including
14 hens two goats and a pregnant lady
and a large basket holding maybe a cobra
judging by the slithering internal noises
also a dozen women chattering in Sanskrit
so we grin at them our universal grin
which means everything and nothing
in high country fit only for mountain goats
I hope the driver drinks nothing but milk
and his helper shrieks for new passengers
at every small town and village firing
A-E-I-O-U like semantic rockets
so I guess Turkish is nothing but vowels
back on the coastal littoral
passing real camels on the highway
"Lookit a real camel" I say
"You ever see a unreal one?" she sez
witheringly to which I say no humbly
and it's spring and all the veiled women
labour in farm fields at one place
we pass 15 mysterious Turkish behinds
planting seeds bending over their furrows
all pointing toward Mecca
at the three-bucks-a-night hotel we find
the toilet is raised footprints and a hole
and no door where I stand guard
when necessary and down the street
passes a wedding or a funeral
I guess the latter the corpse on
a wooden platform kept warm with a blanket
and the bearers bum's rush the dead man
quick into his grave before he can say no

When I can slow down the mind fever
and calm the strangeness to a kind of peace
the place still feels like being on Mars
or maybe Saturn or something and me so foreign
and stupid it's like returning alone
again to earth and alone together
we lie in an uncomfortable bed
and talk to each other comfortingly
and hug each other to sleep

"HAPPINESS"

—searching my memory for it
                    somewhere in the past
visualizing a huge cloudy amphitheatre
full of motionless people and furniture
covered with dustcloths
nothing moving there
until I remember all over again
and the dance begins

happiness?
—the woman whose eyes lit up
as mine must have done
when we made our reciprocal confessions
then a flood of feeling
like continual gifts of lollipops
when you're three years old
which begins to sound silly
—my first radio play
and I sat up half the night
making the requested changes
sixteen other thoughts crammed into
my head and having to choose
exactly the right one
then starting out for Europe next day
some of my last thoughts
still trailing behind the bus
—my first book with Ryerson
which I'd never expected to happen
and maybe the surprise did it
the ache of painful bliss
having come a long way
since morning
and of course
the writing itself
the words exploring
all my veins and arteries

—but that isn't it
not exactly what I mean

for I have felt a sorrow so intense
it could have been called happiness
reverse side of the same thing
—a fear so powerful
that walking was like plodding
deep into the earth all day
and fear leaving me
was like entering cool water
a waterfall in the forest
with only trees watching
—I have written something
and then a year or several years
later felt it nibbling
feel it nibbling nibbling
to be born and finally
become a word like joy
—to feel yourself a conduit
a monster cable
something large and powerful
surging thru my mind
that pays no attention to me
that does not know me
and finishes
leaving me nearly exhausted
discarded as useless
just a convenient pouring spout
while I continue what I'm doing
trying to telephone God
lost in the phone booth

—and by this time
it has become plain to me
that I'm not writing about happiness
at all but the puzzle of being alive
and of feeling all the different things
in all the ages of my life
which is what I've always
written about since the beginning
moving from room to room
in my brain with a guttering candle
peering into the silent places

knowing there is no answer
returning again and again
to the mirror and the tarnished image
of myself

SCHIZOPHRENIA

I am that I am
I have no name for me but me
row and swim
row and swim
through the black sea
the red sea
the brown sea
of earth

And suddenly realize
there is no one but me
in this silica soil
this underground sky
that is part limestone
and 30 percent residual
bones old bones
but I do not know that
my author knows

SELLING APPLES
  Upper Hastings County, Ontario

—driving north
in an old stake truck
loaded with apples
in red October
and after a while
the flying country
of Highway 62
itself began
to seem illusion
and resemble people
instead of landscape

—a lush river valley near Belleville
green fields contain the dimple
in a young girl's face
and I damn near hypnotize myself
searching out human likenesses
farther north at Bannockburn and El Dorado
rock hills beginning to take over
sumac and maple starting forest fires
in the midst of hemlock pine and cedar
a man's face rugged and independent
cheeks red from too much booze and sun
near Bancroft dark evergreen hills
with cloud shadows like sky visitors
emerging from pockets of arable land
unshaven threatening faces
the Shield now dominating everything
Bible Belt country where fathers
and daughters produce near replicas
of themselves in scandalous stories
and pray for their souls baptized
and bathed in the Blood of the Lamb
in the Little Mississippi River

—stopping that night at a Bancroft Hotel
the room a small unpainted box
and Jim my father-in-law an oversized

six feet three inches and once a
17-year-old sergeant in World War I
also native of these barbarous hills
before migration to southern Belleville
he and his wife producing 11 children
child guests in a threadbare world
—myself
managing the difficult feat
of failure at everything I attempted
this more difficult than you might imagine
finally attempting nothing
an only child whatever that means
(of whom a cousin once said "You were
the most spoiled kid I'd ever seen")
my desperation
a bone-tattoo imprinted on the brain
searching for my one true self
and finding many of them

—it must have been in 1917
a shell exploded near the boy sergeant
spraying his legs with shrapnel
a bright day or a dull day and exactly where
it was in France he does not remember
then home
to the pension that dominates his life
with the sick-sweet smell of unhealed wounds
that must be bandaged night and morning
some kind of ointment first
a smell that fills the cheap room
then strips of bandages like puttees
and bed together without talk
our feet projecting from the six-foot bed
as if we'd been climbing a mountain
somewhere and lost our footholds
and sleep in the act of falling

—our apples Northern Spies
grounders from my cousin's farm
(tho he'd been dead a year or two
from a deep soul-sickness picked up

along the Italian boot in the War)
grounders touched by the earth
fresh bruises still concealed
beneath their glowing green-gold skins
apples you contemplate like old wine
and add to each one in that time
the unique flavour of a thousand others
—our idea to sell them cheaply
in the north country boondocks
as if they were only apples

—Herschel Monteagle and Faraday
the windy townships at the tip
of Hastings where it blows so hard
that landmarks change places overnight
river people and valley people
woods runners trappers layabouts
some with faces closed as if they
had long withheld their human selves
others with something exotic
about them like a rare blood type
that makes them dance naked in moonlight
on the night before dying
a fugitive something
that jumps the gap between people
and runs and flows into other faces
—on lost dirt roads like dead end veins
ending in tarpaper shacks unpainted
one-room cabins with three-holer outhouses
and mangy dogs barking in the mud
—for Jim Parkhurst
returning north
was like being born
again every time
where many people still knew him
and he believed they all loved him
and perhaps it was so

—in doorways of sheds and hovels
it was mostly women we encountered
(few of them young for the young

would leave this poverty-stricken place)
their faces lifetime maps of labour
wearing cotton dresses or even overalls
sometimes with faces lighted up
at sight of those bright apples
or sullen because they had no money
and we gave some away to children
—for three days we sold apples
on the last day
a woman's hatchet face forbidding
entrance and cutting off my smile's
intention before it could become
the door about to be slammed hard
and smell of something bad around us
but I didn't ask what it was
and thinking—look behind appearances
and this is the old prosperous middle class
in disguise after financial reverses
some personal misfortunes perhaps
from which no one is ever exempt
and after a long sigh
at the poorest place of all
I glimpse a woman like an elephant
and her daughter a ten-year-old
girl in soiled dress and bare feet
dark hair and so beautiful
the old definitions of beauty
all fulfilled and new ones added
then her face changed
went vacant as a book with blank pages
retarded and left behind elsewhere
and I thought human beauty
cannot exist mindlessly then
she stuck out her tongue at me

—driving south
my spirits lifted and I grinned
inside myself
hill-colours blazed the land drowned
in all the shades of autumn
—those were the bad times for me

and of course all this changed nothing
or maybe it did just maybe it did
when I remembered
that saucy lovely face
in the midst of squalor

In Praise of—

Those guys were big shots
at least I thought so
all the grey suits and pinstripes
on CBC types at 354 Jarvis
—and me right out of the boondocks
wearing my only sport jacket
being force-fed dry martinis
by Bob Weaver and being
introduced to Marshall McLuhan
Austin Willis Robert McCormick
even Morley Callaghan and
whoever came by at the Four Seasons

that was fine in fact marvellous
but the best was Bob saying
"Do you need any money Al?
Just send me some poems
I'll make sure you get the cheque fast"
(I rushed right out and wrote some)
this after living on road-killed rabbits
and Kraft Dinners in the early sixties
my wife and I freezing in winters
that *Do you need any money Al?*
made me realize Bob Weaver was Santa

There were other writers on Weaver's dole
Newlove for sure and Alden Nowlan
and I think Gwendolyn MacEwen
I can't remember all the others
after the thousand martinis we drank
—he wasn't a guy who wanted homage
who keeps you standing waiting
and makes sure you know he's in charge
as different from that as day from night
—and I don't know if he ever got any thanks
or for that matter wanted any
for making the connection
that these rather scruffy human beings
with all the faults of everyone else

were responsible (though very rarely)
for something that leaped from the printed page
dazzled your brain
and fireflies whizzed in the cerebellum

HERSELF

"Sometimes I can feel myself
tossed about in the swirling
currents of your mind
and then—"

"Write that down dear"

—and then sneak around one corner
of the *medulla oblongata*
and leaning against the central
nucleus of the thalamus
you again
But how did all this begin?
—back in a cave somewhere
I regarded your rather pendulous
lower lip and slightly crossed
eyes with unmitigated longing—
How's that again?
Far back in the Pre-Cholesterol
Period of the Mid-Colonic
Age your psyche asserted
itself as a genetic modification
in my scrotum's brain cage
and now
my brain is up to its ass
in social anthropology
and such tenderness as
I have I can never feel
without wondering whether
I should write it down first
or explore this inward melting
feeling that stops just short
of weeping
(pulse rate 75 per minute)

—and now far into old age
with its inevitable conclusion
I am deeply troubled
a profound literary sadness

of knowing I am using death
too much in poems
but turn about
is fair play I guess and
I expect to have it use me
soon for its own purposes
whatever those might be
and it won't be for poems

APHRODITE AT HER BATH

The girl was so beautiful
a man couldn't look at her
directly without turning away
in order to gather willpower
enough to prevent himself
from leaping into that bathtub
—and joining her there

A cousin of my wife's
recently married recently pregnant
I'd fallen in love with her
much too late for anything at all
—and about that pregnancy:
she'd heard somewhere
that booze and a hot bath
would induce abortion
therefore:
my wife leaving us together
before she went to work
in downtown Montreal
Anno Domini 1957
favouring me with a suspicious
glance on leaving the Linton
Ave. apt. in Côte des Neiges
"I'll phone you later
to see if everything's okay"
and I knew just what she meant

Then
splashing in the bathtub
"More beer please"
and cup bearer to the goddess
I fetched a quart from the fridge
(forgot to mention
I made the stuff myself
in a 15 gal. oak whiskey barrel
barley malt and mineral
water bottles supplied by
my pharmacist friend Henry)

—decanting it carefully
to avoid bottom sludge
then sauntering into the presence
of Roman Venus or Greek Aphrodite
(actually I prefer the latter
not to be snobbish about
ethnic origins of deities)
Of course my facetious tone
can't be helped
I was born that way
and abortion is deadly serious
and beauty is its own
excuse for being somebody said
and that girl—well ...

The usual equipment
but arrangement means everything
(God is in the details)
take all the natural things
in the world around us
moonlight on mountain lakes
spring mornings and prairie sunsets
deep sea blue and shore sea green
this girl contained them all:
wearing bra and panties
transparent from the bathwater
she took them off later
as booze removed inhibitions
but no least trace of pinkness
spreading in the bathwater
to indicate successful treatment
At one point I said
"Why abortion?"
and there was a very long pause
not uncomfortable just considering
because it was a serious question
despite these odd circumstances
—and her face that I think could
have peered from a cloud on
the lower reaches of Mount Olympus
turned to me and

meeting her eyes was like drowning
in a field of flowers
the first flowers born in the world
a hundred million years ago

"Why abortion?"

"I woke up in the night
and didn't know what time it was
I did *know* he was beside me
and thought I'd see him there
with moonlight moving across the bed
but when it reached my husband's face
there was no face"

"No face—what do you mean?"

"When the moonlight touched
both of us only I was there"

"Has it occurred to you
that despite what you've just said
about your husband you're
somewhat pregnant anyway?
How did that happen?"

"I don't know
but no one was there
lying beside me in that bed
Do you know what I mean?
How could I have a child
by a man who doesn't exist?"

"But if the man doesn't exist
maybe the foetus doesn't either?"

Cup bearer to the goddess
I kept on feeding her beer
and wanted to ask
"Do you know what you look like?"
breasts so perfect any other

woman would blush to see them
and pubic hair waving underwater
        like flowering seaweed
—but I didn't have the nerve
and thought of it later anyway
I went to change my shirt
for a longer model preventing
certain bulges from showing
And thought again of Aphrodite
in a book of sculpture I had
and looked up the goddess
while buttoning my shirt:
"Aphrodite in Her Bath"
the sculpture by Doidalsas
for King Nicomedes of Bithynia
ruler of a little country in
Asia Minor in the third century BC
—not by Doidalsas directly
this was a later Roman copy
just eighteen inches long
whereas the goddess of Linton
Ave. was about five feet ten inches
—then "More beer please"
and I look at her again:
a thin film of perspiration
beaded on her upper lip
face and body
still untouched by time
in my thoughts a kind of love
the way you look at a flower
a flower you will never see again
in like circumstances
but goddess as well as flower
who will always remain alive
in the bathwater of your mind
"Aphrodite" I said aloud
"More beer please"—and I
obediently decanted another bottle
By late afternoon
I was sampling my own
product along with her

both of us a little sloshed
a little?—a lot
and singing in the bathroom
"Oh my darling oh my darling
Oh my darling Clementine—"

Something awesome about beauty
it lasts no longer than foam on water
but it makes a space for itself in time
wherever it goes
in the mind on the beach in a museum,
even in a bathtub
and after a while it communicates
itself to other things
becomes the sea the sky and mountains
and it remains with me forever
the girl in the bathtub
singing an old song
"Drink to me only with thine eyes—"
of which I remembered
only the first four lines

And now the venue changes
from Montreal to Sidney BC
on the shores of Georgia Strait
Anno Domini 1995
near forty years later
where I sit writing
these words on paper
trying to avoid the eyes
of quite a large crowd
of pro-life demonstrators
gathered threateningly
around this poem

The marriage ended long ago
with two children more or less adult
added to population statistics
Aphrodite herself is 60 years old
(and several thousand years)
and time that is intolerant

of beauty as well as
the brave and innocent
has touched her with autumn
—in the darkness of sunlight tho
or brightly shining moonlight
an immortal goddess still lives
over the long human dying

PICASSO: STILL LIFE WITH SQUIRREL

At Braque's studio in Paris:
the artist working on a Cubist painting
a still life with a package of tobacco
pipe and pack of cards etc.

Picasso: "My poor friend,
this is dreadful.
I see a squirrel in your canvas."
Braque: "That's not possible."
Picasso: "Yes, I know,
but it so happens that I *see* a squirrel.
That canvas is made
to be a painting,
not an optical illusion.
You want them to see
a package of tobacco
and the other things
you're putting in.
But for God's sake
get rid of that squirrel!"

Braque was very dubious
since this was his painting
and he knew what had been
taken from his mind
and there'd been no squirrel
in his mind
therefore there should be
none in the painting
Braque looked again
inside his mind
no squirrel
then looked again
at that painting
very carefully this time
voilà
there it was/is
that damned squirrel

Picasso: "Day after day
Braque fought that squirrel.
He changed the structure,
the light, the composition,
but the squirrel always came back;
once it was in our minds
it was almost impossible
to get out. However different
the forms became, the squirrel
always managed to return.
Finally, after eight or ten
days, Braque was able
to turn the trick
and the canvas again
became a package of tobacco
a deck of cards and
above all
a Cubist painting."

—of course it is still there
the ghost squirrel
just beyond the limits of vision

JACK CORSON

He was small
maybe nine years old
accused at school
of stealing something
I've forgotten what
but a disgrace so awful
it was school gossip
many years ago
—the family moved away
I don't know for sure
but probably for that reason
and Jack Corson and I
we were good friends
we "liked" each other
and I grieved for him
—but now what I felt then
is a very old emotion
the faint smell of dead flowers
at the very most
and not grief any longer
only the memory of it
that has left a little scar
somewhere inside me
I've grown old
and now when a friend dies
the small boy who was
Jack Corson returns to me
to touch this new sorrow
a band-aid from long ago
and death like Monday and Tuesday
sorrow a forgetfulness
of what day it is

MY GRANDFATHER'S COUNTRY
Upper Hastings County, Ontario

Highway 62
in red October
where the Canadian Shield hikes north
with southern birds gone now
thru towns named for an English novel
a battle in Scotland and Raleigh's dream of gold
—Ivanhoe Bannockburn El Dorado
with "Prepare to Meet Thy God" on granite billboards
—light thru the car window
drapes the seat with silken yard goods
and over rock hills in my grandfather's country
where poplar birch and elm trees
are yellow as blazing lemons
the maple and oak are red as red
as a thousand thousand sunsets
refusing darkness entry
to the world

Of course other things are also marvellous
sunsets happen if the atmospheric conditions are right
and the same goes for a blue sky
—there are deserts like great yellow beds of flowers
where a man can walk and walk into identical distance
like an arrow lost in its own target
and a woman scream and a grain of sand will fall
on the other side of the yellow bowl a thousand miles away
and all day long like a wedge of obstinate silver
the moon is tempered and forged in yellow fire
it hangs beside a yellow sun and will not go down

And there are seas in the north so blue
the small bones of the brain take on that same blue glow
like unto a fallen sky
they speak of the illimitable
those immense spaces of nothing and nowhere
the mind can scarcely comprehend
so far beyond human touch we must rely
on impersonal science

to tell us of shimmering violet meadows
and comets visiting earth and returning
                              at such measured intervals
the ancient rememberers were long since dust
and we cry our name to the stars and the stars
do not remember

But the hill-colours are not like that
with no such violence of endings
and earth would appear like a warm red glow
to casual eyes of travellers in space
the woods are alive
and gentle as well as cruel
unlike sand and sea
and if I must commit myself to love
for any one thing
it will be here in this marginal country
where failed farms sink back into earth
the clearings join and fences no longer divide
where the running animals gather their bodies together
and pour themselves upward
into the tips of falling leaves
with mindless faith that presumes a future
Earth that has discarded so much so long
over the absentminded centuries
has remembered the protein formula
from the invincible mould
the chemicals that after selection select themselves
the muscles that kill and the nerves that twitch and rage
the mind-light assigned no definite meaning
but self-regarding and product of the brain
an inside room where the files are kept
and a little lamp of intelligence burns sometimes
with flickering irritation that it exists at all
that occasionally conceives what it cannot conceive
itself and the function of itself:
the purpose we dreamed in another age and time
an end just beyond the limits of vision
some god in ourselves buried deep in the dying flesh
that clutches at life and will not let go

Day ends quickly as if someone had closed their eyes
or a blind photographer was thinking of something else
it's suddenly night
the red glow fades and there is no one here
but myself and I am here only briefly
and yet I am not alone
Leaves fall in my grandfather's country
and mine too for that matter
—later the day will return horizontal and gloomy
among the trees and leaves falling
in the rain-coloured light
exposing for ornithologists here and there
in the future
some empty waiting birds' nests

OUR WILDERNESS

A yellow splash in the green
hill across the water is flowers
and this morning a white plume
of mist floated down from nowhere
inserting itself in the emerald
—our house crouches beside water
a tuck in the landscape
wilderness in miniature
beside a protected salmon stream
and there such marvels appear:
below the kitchen window
sea otters were born
they return recur and reappear
are exiles away from here
and sometimes actually seem
to change into beads of water
and play on the far shore
like circus acrobats
appear to be moving
in all directions at once
whiskered faces comically serious
then all stop as if at a signal
waiting to be interviewed
by imaginary reporters
and ducks kingfishers herons
sometimes raccoon families
switch on our sensor lights at dusk
and caught in the act
they traipse past the windows
like nosey neighbours
on their way to the movies
(and I suppose
in all that nearby underbrush
their babies die sometimes
as human babies do
little burglar faces
twisted in agony
their mothers beside them
in an equivalent of weeping)

Beyond our trees that belong
to themselves the highway
traffic's sullen sounds
a quietness in our bones
we scarcely notice the cars
and underground here
small furred nations
raise their flag in tunnels
below ground
sing anthems at dusk
and we are the aliens here
but at least there is peace
and time's slow passage
the sun a gold coin
from lost Byzantium

In Cannakkale
  Turkey

On the third floor
of the Hotel Anafartalar
beside the Hellespont:
—at midnight a Soviet destroyer
parades by with blazing lights
reflecting in our windows
—close to the hotel site
Leander swam the Hellespont
to meet his girl friend
Hero a priestess of Aphrodite
on the other side
and one stormy night Leander drowned
well within sight of our Hotel
Anafartalar
if we'd been watching
from the window then
—also near here
Xerxes built his bridge of ships
on his way to conquer Greece
in 480 BC
but Greece refused to be conquered
—if we'd been drinking beer at the time
suspended in air in our third floor
room that didn't exist till much later
Xerxes was right under our noses
—and Xenophon passed by as well
around 401 BC
with what was left of his Ten Thousand
bad-tempered and needing a bath
—and Byron dogpaddled across
from Abydos to Sestos in 1810
and made sure everyone heard about it
—20 miles from here
a dozen cities of Troy
all piled on top of each other
dreaming of Paris and Helen
—but I arrived too late
to do anything

but sit beside the Hellespont
and dream about old battles
and book a flight home
quarrelling with my wife
about the date of departure
and whether or not women
are actually the dominant sex

REALISM 2
   —*after Czeslaw Milosz*

Paintings certainly do have
"lastingness"
as Milosz tells us,
but you can add sculpture as well,
and various other works of art,
in fact nearly every human artifact.
As for the people in the painting,
he can "join them" as he says,
even though it's a mental exercise
rather than actual joining,
a trick of the mind—:
but the instant he moves
inside Bruegel's "Winter Landscape"
the "tiny figures skating" stop,
nothing moves,
and when he joins "the choral singing"
in another painting silence falls,
and whatever poetry is vanishes

Something much more mysterious:
take a human action,
choose some kind of incident,
then cut it off before and after,
of course you don't "have it",
but the very fact something occurred
even once makes it eternal,
it cannot be altered or denied:
therefore when Mozart
took a sound out of his head
and with a quill pen
transposed the sound to paper
where it lay silently
and making it infinitely "replica-able"
(a palimpsest of silent sound):
the molecules of eternity
cannot desert *Don Giovanni*
the silent music rehearses

in another dimension
with millions of guest conductors

Therefore I invite Czeslaw Milosz
to join me in listening
to *The Marriage of Figaro*
and stand with me silently
at the graveside in Vienna
and mourn
while they scatter the quicklime
departing as silently
but leaving behind
that essential darkness
from which light is born

MEXICAN VILLAGE

The power goes off
while I'm on the apartment bed
smoking a cigar
trying to write a poem
and the only illumination there is
a little red bud
no bigger than a peso
three inches from my nose
otherwise total darkness
and blackness blacker than light is light
drowns the world
and I switch poems
and write this one
when they come on again
or did they come on again?

It's kinda like the orchid
lost in the Brazilian jungle
it doesn't exist at all
if no one sees it
—did I therefore
cease to exist
when the lights went out
except for a syllogism or two
dirtying the bedspread?

(I'm deadly serious here
no matter how this might seem
there's nothing as serious as humour
when turned around frontwards
it means exactly what it means)

We were all ghosts in that village
i.e. fifty years from now we won't exist
just as what we were then
does not exist now
—it's kinda like the world ends
with a silent sort of whimper
and my two ghosts

are lost between two nowheres
searching for each other
and neither of us exists

I thought you'd stopped being beautiful
but I was wrong
you haven't stopped
and now
in order to hold
my feelings in check
halt the mental process so to speak
slow down the growing physical manifestations
I imagine you with your lower
intestine coiled and looped around your neck
(nobody looks good with the lower
intestine coiled around their neck)
in order to stop
being in love again
which is
fairly
ridiculous
at age
75
most people would agree

Just stand there
blinking like a booby
then glancing at something else nearby
to cover your confusion
the brown necklace now seems to be diamonds
and glitters like a goddess's tears
—but then I'm liable to be
a little distracted at my age
by this sadness inside the body
that feels like triumph in the mind
an extraordinary sensation
and substitute for wisdom
denied the young
I was never capable of before
and unable to put a name to
it may be glimpsed sometimes
but never held

FOR HER IN SUNLIGHT

Didn't turn my head
kept absolutely still
for seven seconds stayed
my fractional life
in this skin tent
until an unpredictable
you has joined me
with river and rain song
and your long quietness
a cloak of invisibility
around both of us
your brown-gold head
turned toward me
and white places
on your hips
are silver
birches on them
        we swing

And this is the way it was:
friends and relations dropped away
the cities blinked out
one by one
and left nothing in their place
but a vagueness
the landscape was dim background
we could see only each other
on the tiny island of us
standing in sunlight
and it was enough
it was enough
—then after a while
the people began to appear again
and they seemed strange to us
we heard the news of the world
and that was strange to us as well
and we glimpsed in each of us
hundreds of dozens of others

in different times and places
                    and mirrors
and glimpse among us
a discovery of strangers and lovers
a collected self

These are life's gifts
and in the loopholes and catacombs of time
travel glance back
to see far-distant replicas of ourselves
perched on a mirage
waving to us
surprised to find us still alive
as if both had imagined the other
as the seed imagines the flower
beyond death
                    the idea we are used to
                    like a far-away train wreck

—scrambling along
the rocky shore
late at night
in zero cold and silence
I stand hesitating
on the armoured lake
ice two feet thick
then hear
the sound of trumpets
clash of cymbals
right under my feet
deep penetrating
my bones' marrow
—lake ice splitting
from shore to distant shore
as if non-human creatures
were communicating
their weird loon-music
bouncing from planet to planet
as if a non-existent god
had sprung into being
in the lake's cold theatre
a terribly noisy deity
had made itself known
to mock a scared atheist
challenge my disbelief
with sensory delusions
evidence of brain damage
(I think of Coleridge
"the ice did split
with a thunder fit"
but Coleridge he
was no help at all)

—it almost goes
without saying
I'm impressed as hell
trapped right in the middle
of a planetary orchestra

silence then trumpets
pause then cymbals
me the guest conductor
and think
my small depressions
my miniscule troubles
what are they anyway
standing here
on earth's mid-navel stone
listening
like an exalted churchgoer
or drunken housefly
escaping
temporarily
the slapping fly-swatter
of an imaginary god

In Mexico

—driving south always south
three or four hundred mile leaps
like a motorized grasshopper
over plains and mountains
skirting cities and crossing rivers
leaves long fled from roadside trees
dead brown grass in meadows
dull sun hung low on a forlorn landscape
storms brewing high in a dirty sky
and south south south
motel to motel to motel
morning frost on motel blacktop
the prone ghost of Canada
and sometimes we looked at each other sadly
who are you?   who am I?
—until finally the pale sun turned golden
the summer solstice double-crossed winter
our cold bones danced into springtime
and orange trees bloomed at the Mexican border

—the hacienda south of Victoria
in Tamaulipas
where we stopped overnight
with suits of armour in the halls
expecting to see Hernando Cortes
in his winter underwear
peering from stone doorways

—driving a ridge road
on the razor edge of mountains
still in Tamaulipas
and fog like grey midnight
all morning
nothing between us and death
a thousand feet down
except the crumbling gravel road-edge
rationally knowing the road *was there*
but the knowledge uncomforting
just guessing your way ahead

nerves popping
the world condensed
to a car-size tin box
and no god available
for rescue purposes

—on every road and highway
road-killed animals
some quite large
even occasional horses
awaiting the carrion-eaters
and where people died
run down by cars and trucks
shrines beside the road
with flowers for the dead
from relatives and lovers
there may even have been
shrines for pet dogs and cats
for all we knew
and it made the highways
into warm human places
except that over everything
circling the sky ceiling
something watching
and if you stopped there
by the road for anything
anything at all
there was a pause
in your own breathing
and high above you
something leaned out

—we had no Spanish
except a few words
for use in stores and markets
and therefore we felt
the peculiar sensation
of not being really there
in other people's eyes
we saw "gringos"
printed on their retinas
as if something vital

had been removed from us
we became abstractions
labelled strangers
possible enemies
beyond friendship
on the human littoral

—noise of feeding in restaurants
each kind of Mexican food
making its own special sound
in the frontal orifice
a protein orchestra
dance of the carbohydrates
and after a while you could identify
tortillas (dry shushing sound)
huevos rancheros   enchiladas
tacos   pimientos   frijoles
chili   (muy caliente)
jalapeños   even more so
—and names the names alone
if pronounced correctly
ignite inside your mouth
—but *cerveza* marvellous *cerveza* (beer)
helados   (ice cream)   dripping from
every inch of a kid's grin
mangos on a stick
flashing yellow signals at the sun

—climbing a steep curving hill
in the Sierra Madres
following a heavy transport
a stake truck rushing down
on us with failed brakes
missing us narrowly
its wheels striking sparks
from the road's stone curb
and faces inside
inside the cab white faces
desperate with knowledge
caught in the act of dying
tumbling end over end
thousands of feet

down the mountainside
—we sat there stricken
with second-hand death
then remembering
cops throw you in jail
for even witnessing accidents
we drove around the transport
and were on our way again
all afternoon
stunned into silence

—in Mexico City
at the high castle
of Chapultepec
where the boy cadets
leaped to their deaths
in 1847
rather than surrender
to the invading Americans
under Gen. Winfield Scott
—I think of the 960 Jews
fighting their last fight
long ago in 73 AD
who leaped to their own deaths
from the hill fortress of Masada
rather than surrender
to the other Romans

—not just poor people
on the streets here
but hungry starving people
beggars in rags
scratching for a living
at the cold concrete
and sometimes nearby
staring vacantly
at absolutely nothing
faces devoid of thought
and after a while
you start to blame them
for having made you feel
so damned uncomfortable

and somehow you owe them
but neither they nor you
know what it is you owe
except that you must take
full responsibility
in your own mind
for not being them

—thinking of Graham Greene
who disliked Mexico
and Waugh who felt much the same
then a bell rings inside me
when I remember the lottery seller
on the Avenida Reforma
face wrinkled as dead leaves
and another ancient in Chapala market
selling iguanas like trussed chickens
old women
they too are Mexico
indomitable as potatoes

—shown over Lawrence's house
near the lake in Chapala
all one hot afternoon
by a real estate salesman
and the estate owner
—transported back to the 1920s
while Lawrence searched for his Ra-na-nim
the great good place
where friends would live in harmony
and everybody be happy
Lorenzo an irritable saint
lungs dissolving and death nearby
but triumphant anyway
in ways impossible to explain

—monster Olmec heads
each of them
taller than a man
on the way to Yucatan
carved by artisans
of a vanished race at La Venta

and they stare at you
from half-closed eyes
indifferently
as if to say
we have seen you
many times before
and will see you again
and all will be the same

—at Acayucan we stopped
"to water the engine's horses"
and passing the local prison
dozens of hands reaching out
from dungeon windows
begging us for money
in order to buy food
and stay alive a little longer
—that night at the motel
rain thundering down
even running under the door
and our electric frypan
blew the motel fuses
and looking outside our doorway
we saw only silver
daggers of falling rain
pounding the drowned world

—stopping at a quiet place
of palm trees and silence
where it seemed human beings
had never been heard of
and being suddenly presented
with the flat blue plate
of the Gulf—such a blue
as jarred the teeth in your head
such a blue

—in Yucatan listening to Babs
from Toronto's Rosedale district
telling a story about
her dead relative being cremated
other relatives taking the ashes

somewhere in deep winter
but getting stuck in the snow
spinning the wheels
        spinning the wheels
finally using their relative
under the car tires
and roaring away
leaving their loved one's
ashes in the silent snow
silent snow

—meeting people from time to time
and sensing that they hated you
and twice somebody saying so
not because you were you
but for being *Norte Americano*
thinking you American
—and to be hated
for no personal reasons
gives one a very odd feeling

—at Chichen Itza
a great city in the past
its long-dead people almost
alive in the present reality of stone
where we are ghostly visitors
—climbing the Toltec pyramid
91 steps to the crowning temple
Eurithe and I holding onto each other
clutching precariously
little jerks of movement
edging toward eternity
("If one of us falls
will it be burial or cremation?")
—seeing the landscape widen
the Mayan-Toltec city
jumps into sunlight
scummy sacrificial pool
emerald jungle beyond
where quetzal birds
fly to their own music

—into a tunnel leading downward
to the Toltec sanctuary
and sprawled at the doorway
a reclining god
Chac Mool
who governs the rain
and a throne shaped like a jaguar
with jewelled eyes
and green jade jaguar spots
—and I think Eurithe and I
I think we feel like children
visiting the future
when we emerge into daylight
to play with our toys
a 1967 Ford Custom
with various travel equipment
in the trunk and some books
parked across the road
from the deserted city
—we look at each other
on our return from the past
"Were we lovers back then?"

—the island of Father Morelos
in Lake Patzcuaro
muleskinner-turned-priest
turned leader of the people
in the Mexican War
of Independence from Spain
executed in 1815
—his statue stands atop the island
130 feet tall with arm upraised
signalling the future
like any ordinary hero
—when we climb the volcano-shaped
island (several hundred feet)
we're much too exhausted
to climb the statue stairs as well
from legs to guts and belly button
heart and head and soul of Father Morelos
dust long ago and far from where

we sit beneath his effigy
and pant for breath
watch fishermen on the lake
below with butterfly nets
and dugout canoes   earning their bread
as their fathers and fathers'
fathers had done
long before Gen. Winfield Scott
long before Hernando Cortes
and the Romans knew they were Romans

—visiting "the place of the hummingbirds"
called TZINTZUNTZAN
onomatopoeia
for darting whirling rainbows
of birds sailing over the town gardens
like tiny coloured angels

—on the Day of the Dead
Nov. 1 and 2
people visit the cemetery
with food and drink and gifts
for their dead relatives
and we huddle around our fireplace
hiding from ghosts in the cold motel
7000 feet higher than the sea
and in the first light of early morn
so difficult to distinguish with
any accuracy the dead
from the living
—but there's such a richness here
that makes you twice alive
that sends you singing silently
Tzin-TZUN-Tzan
and I see clouds of hummingbirds
circling round my dopey head
and Father Morelos blesses me
(an act he'd regret
        if he knew me better)
and during the Night of the Dead
someone leaves two loaves of bread

at our motel room door and "Hey"
I yell after him "we're alive"
but he grins and goes and morning
is a cluster of green and red and gold
and the island of Father Morelos
glows deep crimson and the world
is cleansed and newborn
and we are enthroned
in eternity for now
for this one moment only

—wandering Mexico for ten years
seasonal visitors
beginning to love the country
for reasons one can't believe
are believable
for someone who hasn't lived here
—endless deserts of tree-cactus
many of them
15 or 20 feet tall
with multiple threatening arms
you half expect they'll uproot themselves
and chase you down the highway
and snow-capped volcanoes
shimmering against the sky
cities sweltering in the heat
the sun burning into your head
and then the low moan of rain
(once in Merida in Yucatan
it rained hail like golf balls
we took refuge in a toilet factory
and watched wooden two-by-fours
racing down rivers of rain
in the middle of the street)
and the jungle the Jungle
green that pours into your head
washing over your brain
and the brown people
multitudes of brown people
living in such screaming poverty
you wonder how they can remain silent

and not run around cursing the world
of course they're resilient
but to live and love without hope
of anything better
—or does the same amount of hope
reside in all of us
and you use a small bit of it every day?

—somewhere along the line
in Mexico you think:
is happiness measurable
the same amount available
for all of us?
and your delight in accomplishment
writing a poem you like—say
is that comparable to finding
a crust of mouldy bread
in somebody's garbage can
the same delight?
—is it possible
for one of these *paisanos*
with slack jaw and vacant eye
to be standing alone somewhere
and slowly starting to smile
as I have done myself
all alone and smiling like a fool
knowing how marvellous it is
to be alive?

—sadly there seems no answer
no real answer to anything
only the sea and the land
the beauty of the morning
terror of the night
and a brief residence
here on earth
there is no other place

In the Rain

—approaching a bridge over the Murray Canal
I am seized with a feeling of incompleteness
the desolation of being the last man on earth
and yearning to such a degree that it becomes
a physical illness
yearning like a potato or turnip yearns
or maybe a tall tree in the forest yearns
listening to the silence between raindrops
for a voice to speak in my mind
knowing quite well that I am ridiculous
and stop the car and rush into a phone booth
listening to the ringing sound far from here
listening to the bells ringing far from here

—those few moments waiting
for the receiver to be picked up
rest on a needle point of time
and I will never be here again
but everything I do and say is permanent
unerasable on the blackboard of the instant
on the slate of what was and is and will be
and the word "Hello" in my ears
is a paean an overture and jubilate in the blood
and I hang up without a word

I will sleep my way into death
searching for an instant in dreams
to find that moment again
for that face reconstituted and intact again
with all past ages echoing
from microscopic amoeba to Rilke
culminating in that moment again
on a plastic electronic device
for a rented instant
for a rented instant—

Lady
    with the very modern illness
    agoraphobia
    but ancient as fear
    in a Greek marketplace
Lady
    I have seen your face
crumple and break in ecstasy
of terror of horror of being
alive in this sewer world
feeling alien thoughts beating
at your mind an office desk
protruding from one ear
a subway train from the other
bells clanging gongs shouting
while you're washing the dishes
terror
    of the marketplace
            and falling
falling into that white place
without shadows
    where the rivers are milk
and Lethe dreams
and nothingness has no horizon

        Lady
        I do not say
that underworld is not a good place to be
the land of forgetfulness
where the truly mad with wolf faces
cannot follow
past our floating speck of life on the oceans
from which we emerged bewildered
             and wet
behind the ears
this earth which is a graveyard
built on dead bodies and decayed matter
of all those before us
        animal and vegetable

—but now is the question
                is Lethe better
                tell me Lady?

                        —once on an arctic island
of the Kikastan group in Cumberland Sound
in a moment of desolation
I laid my head flat against island stone
a mountaintop of gneiss and granite
ice floes silent nearby
where I was lost
in the crevices of existence
and I heard the world's heart beating
                        inside the silence
all else an illusion
I heard the singing sound
                        of a stone bird
that flies through the centre of the earth
and I listened

I hear it still
among the nickel-and-dimes people
I know it in the agora
I feel it waiting for that moment
of grace in the unexpected word
the instant that transfigures things
when all your weakness falls away
and your body floats in light

                Lady listen
to sun-song wind-song and song
of the sweeping planets
and the song of the corner grocer
an earth song I heard in the darkness
on an arctic island
from the stone bird flying
through the centre of the earth
                —listen Lady

TRANSVESTITE

Going out naked into the snow
late at night
most unnaturally
   I mean why so silly?
I bet you never did that Julie
      or even in the rain
            women don't
they must wear G-strings
and minimal make-up
because of the Apostle Paul
out there watching
But I'm trying to say why
I do things
       think like that
I can't
only there is an earth-power
in the lazy plunge and swirl of falling things
I don't know what it's for
and somewhere across the neighbourhood lake
a campfire rests against the curve of earth
and touching it the drifting snowflakes
make tiny spitting tasting sounds
and the small furred creatures of the night
      lie under the snow
listening for their enemies

Outside at midnight
in the bright strange air
I have lost and gained myself
rendered invisible
—it's as if I were never here
     had never been at all
     nobody saw me
     tended my wounds
and I did prove I was never here finally
inside the sea inside the silent earth
separate and contained exploding inwardly
the body-clock ticks on
—going outside without

clothes into branching white
coral forests under a sky
surface so many miles over me
the Sky Huntsmen don't know
I'm here and snowflakes falling
back to me are feathers
are cold butterflies
dancing on my shoulders
fused to my broken heartbeat

—so I regained this white plumage

AT AGE 17 I RODE THE FREIGHT TRAINS WEST ACROSS CANADA, travelling from Ontario to Vancouver, BC. I was a non-paying passenger on those trains, a hobo if you like, riding flat cars, boxcars, reefers (refrigerator cars), the couplings between cars, and a few times even clinging to railings on the sides of tank cars until I could reach a safer place, when brakies and railway cops weren't chasing me.

The year was 1936 during the Great Depression, when it seemed half the country was also riding the trains looking for work, along with the inevitable bums and hoboes. Ostensibly I was going west to find a job on the fishing boats out of Vancouver. But at the time, so many hungry men—even a few women dressed as men—were riding the rails, you needed no excuse.

It was my Great Adventure: I was in jail three times, and broke out once; I was lost in the Algoma bush north of Sault Ste. Marie for two days, after a cop threw me off a train; I walked the 38 miles from Golden to Field, BC from sunrise to sunset; and rode through Broadview, Saskatchewan deep in the innards of a harvest combine secured to a flat car, in order to evade Mounties and railway cops. I was 6 feet 3 inches, and weighed 170 pounds. Probably I've never been in such good shape since.

It was dangerous and it was wonderful. Clinging to the narrow catwalk on top of boxcars, moving through high BC mountain country, waving at girls near level crossings. Climbing the switchback rails up the sides of mountains so high the lowest clouds seemed touchable. Then swooping down into sunlit valleys laced with silver rivers ...

Oh yes, it was romantic and it was dirty, but it was rarely boring. Watertanks were scribbled with graffiti, "Kilroy was here" along with descriptions of female anatomy. And the country itself began to take shape in my mind, even if I wasn't entirely aware of this ongoing process. Under those conditions it wasn't an abstraction either, not just names on a map but dirt under your fingernails. Places you've been and people you've known. Afterwards, of course, it's the mind and memory that create our known and loved places, that re-create what already is.

I rode the boxcars west for three years. When World War II began in 1939, I joined the RCAF. Afterwards I worked at all kinds of jobs, in factories, everywhere. And then, during the turmoil of trying to find out who I was and what I was to become, without knowing exactly how it happened, I became a writer. And that was another beginning.

Duncan McLean had been eight years old when he and his family were prisoners of Big Bear and Wandering Spirit during the North-West Rebellion in 1885. When I went to see him in 1971, he was working at Gray's Travel Agency in Winnipeg. I was writing a travel piece for *Maclean's* at that time.

The guy at the travel agency, who looked to be a man of late middle age, told me McLean wasn't in just then. So I went back later and heard the same story. On my third visit I was a little more observant, noticing the man's blue eyes were a little faded. I had a brain wave and said, "You're Duncan McLean, aren't you?"

He didn't even bother denying it, just sort of bristled at me and said, "If you think I'm going to admit that I was a prisoner of the Indians during the North-West Rebellion in the 19th century while I'm selling excursion tickets for air travel to Paris and London, then you're much mistaken."

Of course, he had a point, and besides, the guy didn't look like the 94 years going on a century he must have been. Old Duncan was a snappy dresser, grey pinstripe suit and satin tie making him seem like an ancient man-about-town. And I think he had a date with his girlfriend that night.

McLean remained half-hostile toward me, even while I felt sort of reverent about him. I mean, touch the hand that touched the hands of Wandering Spirit and maybe Louis Riel. This man was Canadian history in the flesh.

After we drank some coffee together, McLean loosened up to the extent of talking about the Rebellion. I wanted to know if he'd felt scared when he was a prisoner; after all, most eight-year-old kids would be. Several whites had already been murdered. McLean, his father, mother (who was pregnant) and sisters were captives of hostile Indians. But the boy who became this rather formidable old man was never afraid.

"There wasn't time for fear. Remember, this was the wild bush country of northern Saskatchewan. We were rushing to join the main body of Indians, and if any of us had fallen behind on the trail, I don't think the Indians would have gone back to look for us—we'd have starved to death." And thinking back in time nearly a century, "I saw one old Indian woman hanging from a tree. She'd killed herself."

"Why?"

"Couldn't keep up with her people. Just too fat and old."

I saw that old woman in my mind, swaying in the cold wind, her body like a pendulum. And then the others went by, the dark faces of Wandering Spirit and Big Bear, names I knew from my high school history books. But these were real people. They looked back at me from McLean's faded blue eyes.

I spent a year in Ottawa in 1967 and '68, visiting the House of Commons and writing about it. As well, I met Marius Barbeau, and lustre attaches to that name! Barbeau was in his early eighties, ethnologist, folklorist, etc. etc., with a whole string of titles after his name. But those titles tell you very little; you have to know the man's career intimately to realize what the word "distinguished" really means.

Barbeau had worked at the National Museum from 1911 until long after his retirement in 1949. He died in 1969. The year before his death, he looked like an elderly Christ, white hair dancing on his forehead. He was, finally, quite unclassifiable.

Immediately after meeting and talking with him, I knew I had to write about him. I did, but what I wrote wasn't nearly good enough; it didn't say that I will never meet another man in this life nearly as alive as Marius Barbeau.

But once, during our several meetings, he was entirely without the dignity that travelled with him and was like a nimbus around that white hair. I was enquiring about his experiences in the Tsimsyan villages of British Columbia's Coast Mountains, Kitwanga, Kispiox, Kitwankool and the rest. He had visited them in the early days of his career, during the First World War and just after, when he was transcribing Indian myths for his National Museum totem pole books. I wanted to know about the Tsimsyan dances in particular. Instead of telling me about them, he offered to show me.

At first he seemed bashful and reticent because I was watching. The room was medium-sized, a dark-varnished dining room table occupied the centre, old fashioned sideboard and antique stuff along the walls. Wearing feathered headdress, moccasins and beaded buckskin jacket, Barbeau danced slowly at first, the soft murmur of his chanting voice filling the room, the drum beating and silence everywhere else. The sound was hypnotic. It stirred something inside me, but I couldn't say why it did. It was like something you might hear when half-awake in the night, unsure about whether or not you might have dreamed the sound.

A little old man who was beginning to forget his visitor, forgetting everything but Rocher de Boule, the mountain at the end of the sky. He danced around the room's obstructions, river waters of the Skeena and Nass flowing swiftly around the legs of the dining room table. Chanting and beating the drum, he danced himself into silence.

I had felt a little embarrassed for him then. Now I'm embarrassed that I was embarrassed. The old house near downtown Ottawa is probably long since torn down, since it was close to modern highrises even then. But in the space where his house once was, I can still think of old Marius dancing, body swaying among the antique furniture; he was one of the ancient rememberers, without whom it is hard to remember our early selves.

On February 6, 1975, two Inuit hunters had set out from their coastal village of Nain, Labrador to trap foxes on an offshore island. They never returned home. Their names were Jacko Onalik and Martin Senigak. The tracks of their blue snowmobile ended at an open lead in the coastal ice of the North Atlantic.

On February 12, I was in Nova Scotia at Canadian Forces Base Greenwood with an Argus air crew from 405 Squadron, listening to weather reports in the briefing room. I had previously convinced an editor at *Weekend Magazine* in Montreal what a good idea it would be for me to go along on an RCAF reconnaissance flight, looking for Russian fishing trawlers and possible submarines invading our coastal waters. Instead, six days after they went missing, we searched for Onalik and Senigak.

The Argus was the noisiest (nerve-shattering) but most reliable aircraft in service in 1975. Its cruising speed was only 180 to 220 miles an hour—but the plane could stay in the air more than 24 hours when necessary. But as aircraft go, the Argus was nearly senile and soon would be only a museum piece.

We fly north over Summerside, PEI, then over the Strait of Belle Isle to Nain. East of the village, the most northerly community on the Labrador coast, we begin our dogleg sweeps over the sea ice. Trained observers—as well as this entirely untrained one—peer from every window. Our altitude remains constant at about 90 metres: we travel 50 kilometres in one direction, then back on an opposite course six kilometres from—and parallel to—our previous swing. Visibility is about three kilometres on either side of the aircraft, and we scan the ice for anything alive. But there is nothing.

The Argus is roaring low over the sea ice when I climb down into the Plexiglass bubble at the aircraft's nose. My body feels terribly breakable as I stare down at the silvery grey mosaic patterns of break-up and then refreezing ice; ice in pressure ridges; ice surrounding rapiers of open water; ice resembling photographs of the moon's grey face ...

Sitting in this transparent bubble, I feel nearly as much a part of the ice below as I am of the aircraft. There's no perspective beneath us; you have to look into the distance like a half-blind bug in order to see the shape of things. I notice my hands are quivering slightly, I think from fear, and yet I also feel exalted ...

In three and a half hours we have crisscrossed more than 3,000 square kilometres of ice. There is nothing to do now except radio the RCMP detachment at Nain, and it will relay word to the Inuit elders: we have failed. The two hunters will never be found. Before leaving this noisy plastic womb, I give way to sentimentality, and mentally send a memorial wreath twisting down to the pack ice below—for Martin Senigak and Jacko Onalik. They did not know my name when they were alive, and there was no reason why they should have. But I will remember them.

You do these things, feel these things, and a transference takes place. Grey ice in the North Atlantic, prairie wheat fields and BC mountains are mapped in the brain, an older section called the limbic brain. It is a strange but also commonplace transference.

August, in the early 1970s. Eurithe, my wife, and I camp our trailer at Batoche, Saskatchewan, on the banks of the South Saskatchewan River. All around us Louis Riel, Gabriel Dumont and the Métis people had skirmished and fought against Major-General Frederick Middleton and the Canadian Militia during the North-West Rebellion. We are parked near the old church, while I read all the books I have on the Rebellion and talk to everyone available. We explore the Métis rifle pits and the graveyard where Dumont and other Métis leaders are buried. And eat our lunch on high hills above the sunlit river.

With small effort you can dream back to that time in the last century, the names whispering in your mind. Did Xavier Letendre with his muzzle-loader clamped under one arm, stuffing gunpowder down the barrel and ramming in a bullet—did he ever pause in the death game to remember running the buffalo at Grand Coteau? The Sioux screaming insults at men from the White Horse Plain? Old Ouellette, age 93, his hearing almost gone, wiping off river mist from his rifle. In a field some distance off, a man rides what seems an inch-long machine that makes dark waves cutting the yellow wheat. And close to where we are sitting: the grave of Gunner Phillips of the Canadian Militia, who died May 9, 1885.

Eighty million years ago, before the Rocky Mountains were born in fire and earthquakes, an 800-kilometre-wide sea extended from the present-day Gulf of Mexico to the Arctic Ocean. In what is now Canada, this shallow sea spread across areas of Alberta and British Columbia. It is called by geologists and others the Bearpaw Sea. This is dinosaur country, where fossilized bones of the giant reptiles have been unearthed from their stone tombs over the past hundred years.

My wife and I have visited Dinosaur Park near Brooks, Alberta and the museum at Drumheller three times, mostly in the early 1970s. We picked up small bits of fossil bone, gaped with other tourists; and once got lost in the badlands when we ignored NoTrespassing signs and left prescribed paths, finding our way back through some rare instinct in my wife's head which she uses instead of a compass.

All around us in the valley of the Red Deer River, buttes, hoodoos and eroded gullies; hills in which time itself is a visible component. Decorating these low hills are narrow strata of coloured rock—bentonite (once volcanic ash), sandstone and other earth elements—which crept imperceptibly into existence over, literally, millions of years. I mean, you are actually looking at time here, although in different form than clock time. Beauty is, I think, impossible of definition, visible only through example. In the badlands of the Red Deer River are the ancient ruins of Earth itself. And they are very beautiful.

The principal attraction for me in Dinosaur Park was "Albert," whose fossilized bones rested in a glass case along the park's tourist road. I gave him the name Albert myself, since it's a handy identity tag. In life, Albert was a seven-and-a-half-metre-long vegetarian duckbill dinosaur, with a bun of flesh and bone on top of his (her?) head, like a prehistoric hairdo. His one distinction from other duckbill dinosaurs was a fractured tail, vertebral bones crushed and broken.

As I looked at that huge broken tail, it occurred to me that no creature would be crazy enough to attack even a harmless vegetarian dinosaur except another dinosaur. My own candidate for such an attack would be the nine-metre-long carnivore *Gorgosaurus*, a slightly smaller relative of the fearsome *Tyrannosaurus Rex*.

So there's Albert, some eighty million years ago, grazing peacefully on tender green salad stuff in shallow waters of the Bearpaw Sea. Then shrieks, roars and howls and hisses, or whatever sounds the big lizards made in emergencies. *Gorgosaurus* had seized Albert's tail in teeth like piano keys and bitten down hard. But the duckbill yanked free, leaving a mouthful of himself behind.

After that, poor Albert's disposition was ruined; even his love life suffered. He had to find his meals farther out in deeper but safer waters. The salad there was tougher and much less delectable. Digestion became more difficult ...

When Albert died much later, moon-tides swept his rotting body back to stinking marshes on the shore of the Bearpaw Sea. Flesh-eaters tore it apart, raising great devil heads in the star-filled evenings, like holes poked in reality. And there's Albert now, at home in his glass case not far from where he lived when alive, identified by his Latin name (which is not Albert) and the date, 1971. And that is a curious form of what might be called immortality.

I remember Angus Mowat and his wife, Barbara, for many, many reasons. They were friends, good friends. But also I remember them for the story Angus told me about watching a man named Scott Hutcheson build a fishing boat on the almost-island shores of Ontario's Prince Edward County. Angus was 17 then, and thought that boat was a thing of beauty, surpassing the loveliness of women. He pedalled back and forth on his bicycle after school from Trenton nearly every day to watch the idea of a boat, invisible in someone's mind, become a nine-metre fishing vessel. Construction was entirely with the old manual tools, some with nearly forgotten names, like the adze, known so well by early pioneers.

Time passed. Angus became a beekeeper, librarian, literary gent (his son also writes) and soldier in two wars. Retired long since, in 1968 Angus was strolling along the same Ontario beach that had been the birthplace of Scott Hutcheson's boat. Surprisingly enough the boat was there—but derelict, a blurred, broken shape, sprouting weeds, with canvas and planking rotten. An old fishing boat, its builder long dead, washed ashore by the waves and clothed in an overcoat of yellow sand.

Angus had the boat hauled from its sandy grave and, drawing on his memory, set out to restore the badly damaged boat to what it had been when he was only 17. But Angus was 75 years old, with one arm crippled by machine-gun bullets in the First World War. He was somewhat damaged himself, and not a very large man either.

But they set to work on the boat, Angus and Barbara. The keel, rotting at one end, was removed; new clamps were cut with a hacksaw. A new oaken keel, 10 metres long, was hewn with adze and sweat—"sometimes by guess or by God, but one of us had to be right," Angus told me much later. "That keel took 27,000 adze strokes. I counted 'em for five minutes, then multiplied that by the hours it took to make the keel."

Nineteen sixty-eight became 1969, and eventually the year turned into summer. Summer became winter, and spring grew tiny coloured jewels on trees. New oaken ribs were cut to shape and steamed to proper curvature, then brass-screwed into place. In 1970, summer removed an ache or two from Angus's old bones. Rotten planks were replaced with new white cedar planking, tapered, steamed and precisely installed. Elm and maple leaves turned red, snow fell, and it was 1971.

One building thought follows another, and the first has to be right or the second, dependent thought can't be. Angus made a mistake. He cut an oaken clamp at the wrong angle. "Maybe I was tired or something. I'd lived that boat for such a long time I thought it would say 'Stop,' and prevent me from making stupid mistakes. I was wrong. And months were wasted."

Arms tired, brain tired and generally discouraged, Angus wondered if this silly dream was a nightmare as he searched his mind for the place he'd gone wrong. It seemed the perfection achieved by other hands was to be denied his own partly crippled hands. In the house Barbara made sandwiches, and he had a drink of rum, resting.

In the sunlight after a nap, as he gazed at the wooden puzzle whose parts refused to fit, a voice said in his ear, "Awful, ain't it?" with sympathy but no hint of condescension. "Take that clamp out and do it again," Scott Hutcheson told him.

"All right, I will," Angus said.

While Angus had been talking to me about all this, I watched the boat at anchor in a little crawl space, rising and falling with the waves. What year? I can't remember. But we sailed across the Bay of Quinte that afternoon, Angus and Barbara, Eurithe and I—a white bird on the wind.

It's one of the pleasures of life that you can skip back in time through another person older than yourself; and through that other, and then, via his or her other, reach back through the centuries. That's what I was doing with Duncan McLean, Marius Barbeau and their others. But it's one-way travel: you can't reach ahead to—whoever's there.

In March and April the daffodils bloom on Vancouver Island. Spring has arrived, the season of birth. People are walking the streets of Sidney, the small town where I spent the last winter. Most of those people will be gone within the next 50 years, as I will too. Just as Angus and

Barbara and others of my friends are gone. Their sons and daughters will replace them, since we are all replaceable.

But we think of the earth, the nearly five-billion-year-old home planet, as something apart from our own mortality. By contrast, love, that emotion of which we speak so glibly, rarely endures more than a few years past its beginnings—at least not in its romantic form. Nevertheless, it's that same love, or something very similar to it, that sends the human race into the future.

On a more cheerful note, I think of that United Nations agency that listed Canada first among the best countries in the world in which to live. I forget how that listing was phrased. It doesn't matter anyway; I knew it all along—the United Nations didn't tell me a thing. I expect it to go on, move forward into the future, a country recognizable as the one I've been talking about here. Its people, of course, will be shaped by time and resemble only distant relations of their forebears. But they will be there, anyway, as all of us will—in shapes we really can't antici-pate, another presence among people on the street, like the memory of a white bird on the wind. The land will remain too. And all of us, the shape-changers, the transitory immortals, evolution's animals, we shall be there as well.

Lament for Bukowski: "perne in a gyre" is a phrase in W.B. Yeats' poem "Sailing to Byzantium." The poet asks the sages to come from their timeless place and guide him at his own point in time. And "the dark gods" of D.H. Lawrence were those which have to do with human sexuality.

Departures: The full names of the people referred to in this poem are: Enid Foody, Tom Marshall, Hilda Parkhurst, Bill Percy and Milton Acorn.

Minor Incident in Asia Minor: poor Joseph has had a bad press for centuries; in fact he's been virtually ignored.

My Grandfather: in this poem Gilgamesh and Enkidu derive from the Sumerian *Epic of Gilgamesh*. Gondwanaland and Laurasia are modern names for the original continents of earth in plate tectonics. They were in existence some two hundred million years ago.

The Names the Names: "they flee from me/that sometime did me seeke" is the beginning of a poem by Sir Thomas Wyatt (1503–1542), in which he mourns the absence of women who used to seek him out. Whereas in my poem I mourn the names of friends I keep forgetting because of old age. Old age? One of my concerns all my life as a writer has been to map and chronicle the passage from youth to old age. In my forgetfulness now, I think there must be another unremembered world in my head, quite different from my consciously known-about-one. And perhaps there are times when the two overlap.

House Party: the poem was written because I thought Rilke omitted some possible aspects of Alcestis that I found interesting.

Picasso: Still Life with Squirrel: the quotes in this poem are taken directly from Françoise Gilot's *Life with Picasso*, page 76.

Realism 2: my poem is a response to one by Czeslaw Milosz in *The New Yorker*, in which he enters imaginatively into the landscapes of some Dutch old masters. This poem has been collected in Milosz's *Facing the River*.

Five poems have appeared in earlier books:

For Her in Sunlight: this poem is considerably revised.

Transvestite: also revised, the original dates back to 1973. The bit about women having to wear G-strings and minimal make-up is, of course, meant to be humorous. Women can do anything they want, and most of them do.

My Grandfather's Country: now revised, and some thirty years since original publication. One verse had bothered me ever since that time. I felt discontented every time I looked at it. Perhaps now I can leave the poem alone.

The Stone Bird: extensively revised and condensed (long-windedness is a besetting fault).

Reassessment: again, much revised.

In Mexico: limited to 50 copies in 1996.

ACKNOWLEDGEMENTS

Quarry
Orbis (UK)
Grain
Southern Review (US)
Queen's Quarterly
Ink Magazine
Imperial Oil Review
The Review
BC Studies
Prairie Fire

And to Sam Solecki, a necessary sounding board and fine editor.

Always to the Canada Council, which has helped me from the beginning.

A.W.P.